LEATHERED

-

MCQUEER

Speculative Books
Glasgow

All Rights Reserved
© Copyright 2018

Illustrations by @pauldock93
Edited by Jennifer Hutchison

ISBN - 978-1-9999180-6-4

www.speculativebooks.net

For my Granny and Granda

ONE

Frank worked in the jail.

As a guard, it was his job to keep the peace in the prison. This wasn't hard for a guy like Frank; 6ft 4, built like the side of a proverbial brick shit-house and a hair-trigger temper–the prisoners regarded Frank with a healthy mix of fear and respect.

Frank had a game he liked to play with a couple of the inmates he liked. The guys he liked were just like himself – hard as fuck. Men who could've had completely different lives if they'd just made better decisions. Frank knew he was lucky he wasn't the one behind bars; he knew that in an alternate timeline he'd have been the one getting locked up at night. The prisoners knew this too and that seemed to be the foundation their mutual respect was based on. The game they played went like this: Frank would name a famous person and ask the prisoner if they thought they could leather them. Then, the prisoner would name a famous person and ask Frank if he could leather them. Sometimes they'd mix it up a wee bit and ask each other who they wouldn't want to fight, who they thought would fight dirty and who, despite having the appearance or personality of a hard man, would be easy to batter. It was widely agreed within the jail that they could all leather Gordon Ramsay.

'Oot ae aw the famous Scottish cunts,' a prisoner called Joe asked Frank. 'Who dae ye hink is the maist handy?'

Frank liked the questions Joe asked him. He once asked Frank if he thought he could take on both The Krankies at the one time, then formulated a plan to take them both on himself. A plan which involved greasing up, Bronson style, and using an unconscious Wee Jimmy Krankie to beat Ian to death.

'The handiest famous cunt in Scotland?' Frank mulled this over while turning over Joe's cell for contraband.

'Ah'd say Frankie Boyle mibbe,' said Joe, running a hand over a slash mark on his face. 'Or Andy Murray's maw. She looks deid behind the eyes. Nae remorse. She wid end ye in a heartbeat if ye ever said anyhin aboot they glaikit boays ae hers. Aw don't look in there mate, eh?'

Too late. Frank was already pulling out an old iPhone from the drawer of Joe's bedside cabinet.

'Fuck sake, Joe, how'd ye get this in here?'

'Joost stick it back, please, mate, ahm beggin ye. It's the only way ah can talk tae mah boay. His maw won't let him come an see me.'

'Didnae know you had a son, mate. Kept that wan quiet.'

'Aye, well, ah don't like talkin aboot him.

There's cunts in here use that kind ae info against ye, know wit ah mean?'

'Aye, ah know, mate,' Frank turned the phone over in his hand. Joe had several Twitter notifications. 'How are ye even charging it? In fact, ah don't want tae know,' Frank put the phone back where he found it. 'Hide it somewhere better next time though, fuck sake. Stevie Wonder could've found that.'

'You're some man, Frank. Right, who's yer hardest famous Scottish cunt?'

Frank pulled off his latex gloves with a snap and said without hesitation: 'Alex Salmond.'

'Salmond? You're aff yer fucking heid. He's soft as shite.'

'Hear me oot. In terms ae politicians–he's the hardest, nae doubt.'

'Wit aboot Mhairi Black?'

'Nah, she's aw talk. Salmond has the air ae a guy that knows nae cunt can touch him. He's goat a confidence, naw, in fact, it's an arrogance he's goat that makes me hink he could leather anybody he wants. Look at the way he struts aboot. He's ugly as fuck but he walks like he's the guy aff the Porage Oats box. He can fight, mark mah words.'

Joe considered everything Frank had said– he'd made a compelling case. 'You're right.'

'Ah know ahm right,' said Frank with a smile, 'ahm always right when it comes tae stuff like this.' He patted Joe on the back and exited the cell. 'Noo hide that fuckin phone, it might no be me that does the next search.'

'You're some boy, Frank.'

Later in the staff room, another guard called Murray tapped Frank on the shoulder.

'You did a sweep of Joe McGuigan's cell earlier, eh, pal?'

'Ah did, aye, how?' Frank asked. He liked Joe but he knew he had a big mouth. He should've taken that phone off him earlier on.

'Well, I found a phone when I was doing my sweep 10 minutes ago. The guy begged me tae let him keep it. Said your pal Joe was allowed to

keep his phone after you found one in his cell?'
Murray had a sort of sleekit smile that always
seemed to be bubbling just under the surface.

'Grassing bastard' thought Frank.

'Ah never found a phone in Joe's cell. Ah've
nae clue wit this cunt's talkin aboot. Sorry, mate.'
Frank went back to reading the paper. Murray
was new in the jail. He was from Edinburgh
and was having a hard time trying to gain any
respect from the prisoners since he was an ex-
copper. Frank hadn't taken to him at all. What
annoyed him the most, aside from the way he
spoke down to the prisoners, was the fact he
insisted on calling Frank 'pal'.

Murray wasn't letting this go.

'I should really be going to the governor with
this. You do know inmates aren't allowed mobile
phones, right?'

'Look, pal,' Frank put down his paper and
rubbed his beard. 'How long have you worked
here noo?'

'3 months now,' Murray shrugged, his bony

shoulders looking they were going to pierce through his shirt. 'Something like that anyway.'

'Surprised ye've no picked up oan this so far but jobsworths don't dae well in here. That kind of stuff might go doon well in the polis but no in here. Ye don't want tae be making enemies, or annoyin the governor wi every wee hing ye find in a cunt's cell.'

'But it's not allowed.'

'Did you no listen ae wit ah just said tae ye there? The guy's using that phone tae talk tae his boay, fuck sake. Noo, let me put it this way – keep this shite up and you'll get leathered. An if ye keep annoyin the other guards, it might no be aff a prisoner.'

'Are you… threatening me?'

Frank stood up, breathing in and blowing himself up like a puffer fish. 'Ahm just tryin tae keep ye right, pal.'

Murray backed off and went to sit by himself. 'You know he doesn't have a son, don't you?' he shouted over as a parting shot to Frank.

'Wit?'

'Just trying to keep you right, pal.'

Frank went back to work.

'Hawl you,' Frank shouted as he walked over to the pool tables. Joe kept walking round one, trying to keep a bit of distance between him and Frank.

'Frank, big man, ah never said anyhin tae anycunt ah promise,' Joe blubbed.

'C'moan wi me,' Frank grabbed Joe by the neck of his jumper. The other prisoners fell silent.

Marching Joe up the stairs to his cell, he passed by Murray. 'Anymare ae your shite,' he seethed at him, 'and it'll be you ah come fur next.' Murray gulped and kept walking.

Frank flung Joe into his cell.

'Where's that fuckin phone?'

'Frank, mate, ahm sorry. Ah didnae mean ae tell anycunt, ah swear.'

Frank rifled through all of Joe's possessions, turning the cell upside down, cans of Lynx deodorant thrown against the wall in frustration as he searched frantically for the phone.

'You took advantage ae mah kind-hearted nature, Joe. Where's the fuckin phone?'

'Please mate, ah need it tae talk tae mah boay.'

'You've no goat a fuckin boay!' Frank launched Joe's wafer thin mattress across the tiny room.

Joe was about to refute the accusation when he saw how tightly clenched Frank's fists were. He was about to blow.

'Right, awrite. Ah've no goat a son.'

'AH FUCKIN KNOW THAT! GIE ME THE PHONE!' Frank started ripping off the posters Joe had on his wall in case he was hiding the phone in a Shawshank Redemption-style cubby-hole.

'Frank... Frank,' Joe pleaded but Frank ignored him and kept flinging his meagre possessions around the cell. 'Frank, listen ae me fur a minute. FRANK!'

Frank stopped what he was doing. No

prisoner had ever raised their voice to him before. Maybe he was losing his touch.

'Ye'll no find the phone in here, mate.'

'How no? Have you gave it tae somecunt ya sneaky wee fuckin RAT?'

'Naw. Ah've no. Ah might look daft but ahm no that stupit.'

Frank rubbed the bridge of his nose then nodded for Joe to continue.

'Ye'll no find it in the cell because,' Joe poked his head out into the corridor to see if anybody might hear what he was about to say. He lowered his voice to a whisper and closed his eyes. 'Because… it's up mah arse.'

'Ya dirty bastard, could ye no joost hide it somewhere in yer cell?'

'Well, you telt me ae hide it somewhere better. So ah did.'

Frank reached into his back pocket for a pair of latex gloves. He always kept a pair handy for occasions such as this. He never underestimated just how manky prisoners could be. After pulling them on, he nodded solemnly at the door, instructing Joe to close it over.

'Ah need that phone aff ye, mate. Clearly yous cunts think ye can take me fur a fuckin mug. Think ahm soft, aye? That wit it is?' Frank advanced on Joe who had backed into a corner.

'Naw, Frank. Ye know nae cunt hinks that. Yer the hardest cunt in here.'

'Aye, an you basturts wid dae well tae remember that. Drap yer drawers, squat, an spread yer cheeks.'

'Frank, can ah no joost pull it oot masel? This is a bit… undignified.'

'Can ye fuck!' Frank barked. 'Squat.'

Joe lowered himself into a squat. 'This low enough?'

'Perfect,' Frank said as he knelt down so he was in line with Joe's arse. 'Spread.'

Joe did as he was told. As he pulled apart his cheeks, it looked like a cheese toastie being opened up.

'Ye might've cleaned yer arse, Joe. Jesus

Christ.'

'Well ah didnae hink anybody wis gonnae be poking aboot doon there, did ah?'

Frank screwed up his face and tentatively reached in and grabbed the edge of the phone between his index finger and thumb -Joe's sphincter pulled back.

'Yer gonnae need tae relax a bit.'

Joe did as he was told and the phone slid out. The elasticity of the anus and the capacity of the cavity never failed to amaze Frank–even after years of watching prisoners pull various weapons, drugs and phones out of their arses.

Frank wiped away some shite from the screen and turned it on. Straight away it started displaying countless Twitter notifications.

'So ye've no been using it tae talk tae yer boay. Ye've been fuckin tweetin?' Frank shook his head. 'Wit nonsense huv ye been spoutin oan Twitter?'

'Well,' Joe was looking very chuffed with himself as he pulled his boxers and joggie bottoms back up. 'Ahm quite active oan the auld Twitter. "Twitter famous" they call me.'

'"Twitter famous"? Fuck dis that mean?'

'Well, obviously, in here ahm joost Joe, right? But see oanline, ahm JailBhoy67. Ah joost tweet aboot life oan the inside an aw that. Folk love it.'

Frank pretended to be impressed. 'Think ah might get Twitter then. Ahm sure you must post some rivetin content, eh? Aw look at me,' he did an impersonation of Joe's nasally voice. 'Ahm JailBhoy. The day ah played pool, ate mah dinner, then went tae bed. Same as ah've did every day since 1998. It's fuckin tragic.'

'Hawl that's harsh. Ahm an interesting guy. Ahm underappreciated in here, ye know. Cunts oanline love me.'

'Ahm sure they dae, mate. Ye know wit?' Frank tossed the shit covered phone back to Joe. 'Joost keep the phone. Yer no up tae nae good wi it. Yer joost a bit ae a sad act. Nae offence.'

Joe waved his hand dismissively. He went over to his toilet and started cleaning the phone.

'Ye should gie Twitter a go, Frank, ahm tellin ye, mate. It's class.'

'Ah don't hink so, mate.' Frank pulled off his gloves. 'Ah've no goat much tae talk aboot. Ahm either in here wi you cunts or ahm in the hoose watching the telly.'

'Ye could talk aboot cunts ye could batter. Ye can set up wee polls an that. Get yer followers tae vote oan who they think they could batter an aw that.'

Frank actually quite liked the sound of that. 'Ah'll see, mate. Ah'll see.'

•

Later that night, lying on the couch at home alone, Frank switched the telly over to the 10 o'clock news.

'Good evening. The North Korean leader Kim Jong Un's continued threats towards the United States and its allies could soon spark a military reaction from US President Donald Trump, according to a nuclear deterrent expert…'

'That's plenty,' Frank said to himself as he put

the telly on mute and picked up his phone.

Fuck it, he thought. Ahm joining Twitter.

The first thing he did after setting up his new Twitter account was to look for Joe's profile. He was stunned to see that Joe, somehow, had over ten thousand followers. Frank laughed to himself as he read through Joe's tweets:

Day 7,399 in the big Bar-L hoose – Joe had his iPhone forcibly removed from his arse but the kind guard allowed him to keep it instead of handing it in to the governor when he heard about yer auld da's exploits on Twitter #Legend

Day 7,399 in the big Bar-L hoose – getting really fuckin good at playin pool oan a wonky table.

Frank wracked his brains as he tried to think of a witty reply to Joe's musings. He settled for: Joe, fuck up and go to bed.

Joe replied with a sad faced emoji.

Frank followed all of the usual people folk follow when they first join Twitter. The likes of Donald Trump (Not that he was a fan of him, in fact Frank hated him, he just wanted to see the mad shit he tweeted) a few footballers and a couple of actors and singers. Scrolling through his feed a notification popped up, Why not send your first tweet, Frank? Frank didn't know what to say. He looked up at the telly. Kim Jong-Un's big ball face filled the screen. Ah could leather him, thought Frank. So he tweeted:

Kim Jong-Un? I could kick fuck out of him.

TWO

At the same time as Frank hit send on his first tweet, a payroll administrator by the name of Cho was waking up in Pyongyang, North Korea. Before she left for work she had a quick check on the phone she kept hidden in her house, in a similar fashion to which a certain Mr Joe McGuigan, residing in H.M.P. Barlinnie, Glasgow, kept his. Despite Twitter access being blocked in her country, Cho had managed to gain access through her clever use of proxy servers and tapping into the 4G signal of South Korea. As she did every morning, she typed the name of her country's leader into the search bar to see what the western world was saying about him. The first tweet she saw was from a Mr. Frank Curran of Garthamlock, Glasgow:username "@HardCunt72". It read: Kim Jong-Un? I could kick fuck out of him. For Frank, this was just a throwaway sentence. He typed it out, hit send and went to bed, forgetting what he'd just tweeted almost instantly. For Cho, this tweet would be what she would use to undermine her leader, his nefarious regime and start a revolution.

She took a screenshot of Frank's tweet and stored the phone safely back in its hiding place under the floorboards. As a child, she'd witnessed her neighbours dragged away to a labour camp in broad daylight. South Koreans would launch videotapes filled with news reports, adverts, soaps, documentaries and films over the border into the North. These tapes were distributed and smuggled throughout the country by dissidents to show that life outside North Korea was better and not the cesspit the regime wanted people to believe it was. One of these tapes found its way to Cho's neighbours, an elderly couple. They watched the tape out of curiosity, knowing if they were caught with it they were as good as dead. The Secret Police were aware of the tapes being moved around the country and started cutting the electricity before carrying out raids of people's homes and inspecting their video players. It was during one of these raids Cho's neighbours were caught, beaten and hauled away. The image of the old man and woman in tears being dragged apart into vans by a team of policemen had lived with her ever since, always there in the back of her mind.

Cho met up with her friend Ri after work that day and told her about Frank's tweet.

'Ri, there is this man in Scotland,' she said excitedly as they walked home. 'He said on Twitter he can "kick fuck out of" Kim Jong-Un!'

Ri, although a dear friend of Cho, was very concerned about her rebellious ways. Ri had seen her own parents hauled away by the Secret Police just a couple of years ago. She was terrified she was going to lose Cho in the same way.

'Please stop this,' Ri pleaded. 'We have a good life here. We aren't starving, we aren't in dire poverty, things aren't that bad.'

'Yes, we're okay. But what about everyone else? People get dragged away for nothing. People are dying every day of starvation but I'm not allowed to say anything because I'm okay?'

'Cho, keep your voice down,' the two women were walking home down a busy street and people were starting to notice Cho getting animated.

'Okay. Okay,' Cho said, lowering her voice. 'But you must see that Kim Jong-Un is a laughing stock outside of this country. Everyone here thinks he is the great, supreme leader when really he's just an overgrown child. I wish there was a way to show everyone what the world really thinks of him.'

'You're playing with fire, Cho. Please be careful.'

As they approached Ri's apartment building

they said their goodbyes. 'Get home safe and be careful,' Ri pleaded once again.

'I will,' Cho replied. However, Cho wasn't heading home, she was heading to meet up with her fellow would-be revolutionaries. They met once a month in the staff room of the Lucky Lane Bowling Alley, whose manager was a staunch opponent of the country's regime. Only the most patriotic citizens could live in Pyongyang and to any observer, Cho and her comrades were just that. Cho and her female pals, Kye and Myong, kept their hair tied up, as was the law, and wore sensible clothing in muted colours so as not to draw attention to themselves. While the men, Tokko, Sol and Hyang, wore their pin badges of the late Kim Jong-il and Kim Il-Sung and government approved haircuts with apparent pride. Once they were safely in the confines of the staff room, their base, the women were free to let their hair down and the men removed their badges from their lapels, placing them by the portrait of Kim Jong-Un on the wall.

'First order of business,' Hyang, the manager

of the bowling alley said, 'I've received word from my friend in Ryonggang that the food situation there is dire. We're hoping another group is going to help them out, but, if it comes to it, will any of you be willing to go and drop off some food?'

The mood in the room changed instantly and the rest of the group looked at the floor to avoid making eye contact with Hyang. A trip like this was basically a suicide mission.

'No takers? We probably won't have to go, but it'd be nice to let them know they have people here able and willing to help them.'

Cho meekly raised her hand, still staring at the floor.

Hyang nodded in approval. 'That was a test,' he said, 'and you all failed. Apart from Cho, of course.'

Cho swelled with pride.

'Anyway, tonight I was thinking we could come up with ideas for more flyers and posters and stuff like that. Cho, any ideas? Have you seen anything we could use on that dodgy phone of yours?'

'I have actually. We all know everyone outside of this country thinks Kim Jong-Un is an idiot, right?'

The group all nodded in agreement.

'Well, we need to let everyone else know this. There's this guy in Scotland who said on Twitter, and I quote, that he "could kick fuck out of him".'

The group were excited to hear this.

'Does he look as if he could?' asked Tokko.

'Yes! He's like a monster! I'm going to try and find out some more about him tonight.'

'We should get that tweet on a poster,' said Myong.

'We should,' said Hyang, looking deep in thought. 'I can see it now – a picture of this guy standing triumphant over a lifeless Kim. He can be our poster boy.'

'Cho, get us a picture of him for tomorrow night and I'll get the posters made ASAP. This is the kind of thing we've been waiting for,' said

Tokko, the poster guy. 'This will show everyone here how weak Kim really is and how easy it will be for us to take back our country!'

Cho headed home that night filled with a new optimism for the future. Feeling as if, with Frank's help, she and her group could really change things for the better in their country.

THREE

A few days later, Kim Jong-Un was sat in his massively oversized chair at his equally oversized desk. He hovered his hand over the big red button, the button that would launch nuclear warheads towards the USA and almost certainly bring about WW3, if not Armageddon. He decided against pressing the button today, he'd see how he felt tomorrow. He moved over to the massively oversized mirror and admired his massively oversized self.

His closest aide came running into the room. 'Supreme Leader, we have seized a large quantity of posters printed by a dissident group here in Pyongyang.'

Kim sighed, he was busy admiring his haircut in the mirror.

'Supreme Leader, they are making outrageous and defamatory claims about you.'

Now he had Kim's interest.

'What are they saying?' Kim began to vibrate with rage but still faced the mirror. He eyed the poster in the aide's trembling hands.

'Well the group themselves aren't actually saying anything. It's someone else. A man from Scotland. He's saying he could "kick fuck out of you".'

'Let me see the poster.'

'Supreme Leader, I don't think you should.'

'GIVE ME IT!' Kim barked, spinning round and snatching the poster from his aide's hand.

The poster had Frank's profile picture from Twitter: him in his gym gear, flexing a tattoo covered arm, photoshopped to show him standing over a lifeless Kim Jong-Un who lay on the deck. The text read:

The Young Master? The Great Successor? Outstanding Leader?

Don't think so!

Kim is the laughing stock of the world.

Frank from Scotland says he will 'kick fuck out of him!'

The poster was signed off by the 'North Korean People's Resistance'. There was also a few screenshots of Tweets from other Scottish people:

Actual cannae believe the state of that Kim Jong-Un's hair.

Kim Jong-Un is like a big, massive, overgrown baby.

Mad Kim fae North Korea looks like he's made oot ae Billy bear ham.

'Who made these?' Kim asked. Flecks of spit landed on his aide's face as he seethed out the words.

'We're not sure, sir.'

'Well how many of these have you seized?'

'Thousands, sir. But they're still everywhere. Look,' the aide turned to the wall of television screens in Kim's office. He hit a panel next to them and displayed multiple live feeds from across Pyongyang. The posters were everywhere. Hanging on walls, strewn across pavements, pasted onto windows and any other flat surface Cho and her gang could find. The electricity in Pyongyang tended to be cut after 10pm so her and the rest of her dissident pals had snuck out and plastered them everywhere under the cover of darkness.

'This is outrageous!' Kim screamed. 'Find this man called Frank. I want to fight him.'

'Sir, we could just take down the posters and imprison anyone who-'

'I said I want to fight him, did you not hear me? I could fight him and win. It will quash all of this resistance nonsense.'

The aide looked at the poster. It was hard to tell from the picture but he was sure Frank definitely looked taller than Kim. And he was definitely stronger, there was no doubt about that.

'Is that a… *wise* idea, sir?'

'Of course it is, I'm Kim Jong-Un! I could fight anyone!'

The aide thought to himself that Kim looked as if he could barely fight sleep. The man got out of breath walking to the toilet.

'Sir, please reconsider this…'

'Are you disagreeing with your Supreme Leader?' Kim took a step towards his aide. He was toe-to-toe with him. The aide bowed his head in subordination and let out a little whine.

'N-n-n-no, sir,' although the aide knew Kim couldn't possibly fight Frank, he was still bigger and stronger than he was.

'Send a delegation to Scotland and find this Frank character,' Kim said in a low growl. 'When you find him, let me know straight away and I'll fly out to fight him. We need to show the western world that North Korea takes threats like this very seriously.'

'Yes, sir,' replied the aide as he scuttled away.

FOUR

Frank, unaware that he had become a symbol of the North Korean people's resistance against their oppressive regime, sat outside the jail in his car. He was starting to get fed up with his job. Over the last few days, he'd realised that his life wasn't much different from the prisoners he locked up at night. The only difference between him and the likes of Joe was that Frank got to go home at the end of the day. Home to do what though? Sit about, watch some shite on the telly, go to bed then get up the next morning to go to the jail again? What kind of life was that? He was as much a prisoner as anyone behind those bars. 10 years he'd worked there. Frank looked out at the ominous structure of the prison. Everything about it made him feel depressed. The weather-beaten brick work, the barbed wire, even the rusty gates; it was as if every aspect of its design was tailored to make him feel like all the hope and joy in his body had been leached out of him. *If any cunt gies me any shite the day*, he thought to himself, *ahm tellin them to ram their joab up their fuckin arse.*

At lunchtime, Frank was sitting in the staff room on his phone, still in a bad mood from before. His morning had been relatively uneventful. He did his rounds, a couple of random cell checks and some basic paperwork– all without any hassle from anyone. When Frank was in a bad mood the prisoners knew not to even look at him, never mind talk to him. The same went for the other guards.

He flicked through Twitter. He'd gained thousands of new followers over the last few days and his mentions were filled with hundreds and hundreds of tweets written in Korean. Frank assumed it was all just spam, truth be told it was starting to annoy him, and he was thinking about deleting the app. Then a tweet written in English with a picture attached to it caught his eye. It was from Cho and it read:

Frank! You are our hero! Thanks for showing how weak our leader is!

As Frank opened the picture his jaw nearly hit the floor. 'Wit the fuck,' he said to himself. There were articles from South Korean news websites talking about the posters as well. Frank thought he must be the victim of an elaborate wind up. Maybe it was Joe, he thought.

'Frank,' Murray said, popping his head into the staff room. 'You're wanted in the governor's office, pal.'

'Wit fur?'

'No idea. But there's a load of guys in suits in there as well.'

'Have you grassed oan me, ya prick?' Frank got up and grabbed Murray around the tops of his arms, pinning them to his side. 'If you've grassed oan me ah swear tae God, pal, ah'll fuckin kill ye.'

'Frank, honestly, I haven't said anything.' Murray blubbed, he felt as if Frank was about to burst his biceps to open. 'I promise.'

Frank let go of him. He didn't like Murray even in the slightest but he could tell he wasn't a liar. Murray looked shellshocked and rubbed his arms, trying to ease the pain in them.

'You've nae idea wit this is aboot then?' Frank asked Murray.

'If I did,' Murray gulped, 'I would tell you.'

Frank chapped the door of the governor's office. The governor opened the door slightly, his tight-lipped expression looked like it had been carved into stone.

'Come in, Frank.' he said quietly, ushering Frank into the room. Frank was met by the faces of three people he didn't know – a Korean man and woman and a guy he thought he recognised from the telly. The three strangers sat in front

of the governor's desk with two empty chairs
sitting out as well.

'Frank this is a most unusual situation we
find ourselves in,' the governor said. 'Most
unusual indeed. Please sit down.'

Frank did as he was asked and sat down
with the guy from the telly on his right and
the Korean couple to his left. The guy from the
telly smiled at Frank but the Koreans kept their
eyes set dead ahead. They sent a shiver through
Frank's body. The governor sat down as his
phone rang.

'Okay, send her up,' he said down the line.

'Wit's happenin here?' Frank asked.

'I'll tell you when this woman gets here. That'll
be her now actually,' the governor said as there
was a knock on the door. 'Come in,' he shouted.
In walked a woman, around 60, flanked by two
burly security guards in sunglasses. The Koreans
turned around, drew their eyes off her as she
offered them her hand, and returned their gazes
to the back wall of the office. Frank thought

they were acting like robots or something. The woman took the last remaining seat while her guards stood with their backs to the door.

'Is this aboot Joe McGuigan?' Frank asked the governor. He thought he had what was happening here all figured out, this was an inquiry into why he didn't report the fact he knew Joe had a phone. He remembered he'd replied to one of Joe's tweets the other night. 'Fuck,' he said as the governor pursed his lips and leafed through some paper. Frank was sure he was about to lose his job.

'Frank, while what happened with Joe is a regrettable incident which we should really be taking further,' the governor said. 'There are bigger matters to attend to.'

'Much bigger,' interjected the guy on Frank's right. 'I'm Mark, by the way, Mark Dallas.'

'You the cunt fae the wrestling?' Frank asked.

'Aye,' Mark replied, flashing Frank a smile. 'The one and only.'

'Ahm a wee bit confused here, mate.'

'I'll let your boss fill you in.'

'Yes, this is Mark from the wrestling and to your left are two delegates from North Korea,' said the governor.

'Awrite,' Frank said leaning over to shake their hands. The delegates ignored him.

'They don't say much. Don't waste your time, Frank. This, however,' the governor gestured to the woman who'd just entered, 'is Katherine Muir, head of MI6.'

'Ooft, like the spy mob?' Frank asked, shaking her hand.

'Yes, something like that,' she smirked.

'Right. So there's me, a cunt fae the wrestling, a spy and two cunts fae North Korea? This isnae aboot Joe is it? Unless… Joe's really a spy?'

The governor gave a chuckle. 'Of course he's not, Frank. This is all about you. You're… somewhat of a celebrity in North Korea now.'

Frank looked to his left. The two North Koreans were staring at him. They looked raging.

'Ah've noticed ah've goat a few followers oan twitter that write in Japanese or suttin. Am ah… Twitter famous err there?'

'You are a threat to the regime and must be destroyed,' said the Korean woman. The quietly threatening manner in which she said it gave Frank the fear.

'They're not Japanese,' Katherine said. 'Your followers are North Korean. You've became a symbol of the North Korean People's Resistance group. They've been using your image on posters after you said you could "kick fuck out of" Kim Jong-Un.'

'Aw aye,' Frank laughed. 'Ah mind ah tweeted that. Ah could, by the way, joost sayin.' He looked over the North Koreans who were sitting with their fists tightly clenched.

'Well that's the thing,' Katherine got up and motioned for one of her guards to pass her the envelope he was holding. 'Kim Jong-Un wants to fight you. And we think this could be a good thing.'

Mark patted Frank's leg. 'You're gonnae be a star, big man. I'm gonnae organise the fight. I can see it now, in the Hydro. Pay-per-view. It'll be bigger than Mayweather and McGregor.'

'The Supreme leader will CRUSH you,' said the Korean man, slamming a fist on the governor's table.

'This is a wind-up, eh? Awrite, good yin,' Frank said standing up. 'Where's the cameras? Wit's this fur? The telly? Some mad hidden camera hing? In fact,' Frank moved over and stood behind the North Korean delegate's chairs. 'This is Ant an Dec, int it? Ahm oan that Saturday Night Takeaway! Haha, when's this gawn oan the telly then?'

'Frank, sit down and shut up,' said the governor. 'This is serious business.'

Frank sat down.

'This is fur real?' he asked. Everyone in the room nodded.

'The Supreme Leader wants to fight you to remind the western world of the strength of the

Kim dynasty. It's time you gave us some respect. We could wipe out this country at the drop of a hat you know,' the woman said.

'Frank,' said Katherine, 'If you fight him and win, which we're pretty sure you will, you could give a lot of hope to the North Korean people who are against his regime. The man is a monster.'

'Wit you sayin ae aw this?' Frank asked the governor.

'Well, you've not got much choice, really. I have to terminate your employment here anyway so you'd be as well…'

'Wait, hawd oan a minute. How come?'

'Talking to prisoners online. Withholding knowledge of contraband in a prisoner's cell. These are serious offences, Frank. I've no choice in the matter.'

'Never you mind yer joab here, mate,' said Mark. 'Bigger and brighter things await you, Frankie boy. Yer a big handsome strapping bastard of a guy. A career in the auld wrestling or maybe cage fighting wid be better. Wit d'ye say?'

Frank sat open-mouthed. He didn't know how he was supposed to feel. In the space of a few minutes he'd been sacked, offered a new career as a wrestler and been asked to fight the dictator of North Korea. It was a lot to take in.

'Ah… ah… ah don't know wit tae say here,' Frank said.

'Say aye, ya mad man!' said Mark.

Katherine nodded at her guards again and one of them came over with a piece of paper.

'The government has drawn up this contract for you to sign,' Katherine said as the guard handed Frank the paper. 'It's nothing too serious. It just says you can't sue the government, for example, for any injuries sustained. Kim Jong-Un will be signing something similar. He's very excited about the fight, we hear.'

'This is yer contract fur the wrestling as well, mate,' Mark handed Frank a piece of paper.

'HAWF A MILLION QUID!?' Frank

exclaimed as he read over his agreement.

'Aye, that's right. It's aw yours. If ye win that is.'

'Ah will, don't you worry aboot that. So when's the fight?'

'Two weeks today,' said Katherine.

'Buzzin fur it,' Frank said as he stood up. 'Better go an start trainin then, eh? Wit's the deal, is it boxin or wrestling or wit?'

'Bareknuckle. Don't worry though, we've goat the best ae the best lined up tae help ye oot, Frank. Guys that've worked wi Conor McGregor, Anthony Joshua and, eh, Scott Harrison. You'll go right through this cunt. Moan, we'll head straight tae the gym,' Mark said, putting an arm round Frank.

As Frank opened the door to the office, the governor shouted after him.

'It's a shame we've had to let you go, Frank,' he said. 'Your p45 will be posted out to you.'

'Wi aw due respect, chief. Shove yer joab up yer arse.'

As the governor shook his head in disapproval, the Koreans made a throat slitting gesture in perfect sync.

'Tell Kim he's getting fuckin leathered,' Frank said to them.

FIVE

The fight was announced straight after Frank signed his contracts. In North Korea, Cho was so excited when she found out she thought she was going to be sick. Posters were put up everywhere by the state, glorifying Kim Jong-Un, of course. Some portrayed him standing over an unconscious Frank, others him wiping his arse with a saltire flag and others depicted him with the Loch Ness Monster in a headlock. Giant screens were erected all over the cities and the fight was to be available to watch on everyone's television in the country. Viewing was mandatory.

'I basically made this happen!' Cho said excitedly to Ri. 'If Frank wins, who knows what it'll mean for the future. Oh! Maybe Frank will KILL him, what would happen then? Would the regime be finished?'

'Who knows,' said Ri, she was barely listening to Cho as they walked down the street.

'Are you okay, Ri? You don't seem very enthusiastic about the fight.'

Ri sighed and turned back to watch the sun set behind a high-rise.

'I'm leaving here,' she said, without making eye contact with Cho.

'Oh, that's nice,' Cho smiled. 'I mean I'll miss you but we could still see each other at the weekends or something, I suppose. Have you got a new job?'

Ri sighed again. She looked down at the ground as a teardrop fell from her eye. 'I'm defecting. I'm going to live in the South. My uncle can get me across the border, he says. My father's family are all there.'

'I didn't think you had it in you,' Cho laughed. 'When do you leave?'

'Tonight.'

'Tonight!' Cho shouted, a traffic policeman cast them a mean look.

'Yes, tonight. Come with me.'

'Ri, I can't. I…'

'There's nothing for us here. Especially you, Cho. How long before the secret police uncover you and your group? How long before you're dragged away to a labour camp in the middle of the night? How long before…' Ri was crying now. 'How long before you get killed?'

Cho held her tight. 'I'll be fine. This fight could change our lives here.'

'It won't.'

'Move along!' barked the traffic policeman from across the road.

'We're in the middle of something!' Cho shouted back. The policeman reached for his baton.

Ri grabbed Cho by the wrist and dragged her away.

'I'm keeping an eye on you two,' the policeman shouted after them.

Round the corner and out of sight, Ri put her hands either side of Cho's face and brushed some hair back behind her ears.

'I won't beg you. Just please come. Meet me here at midnight if you change your mind.'

'Ri, I want to bring down this regime. I can't do that anywhere else but from here. Did you not see all the posters we put up? Tokko says he's had hundreds of people wanting to join the group. We are giving people hope here! People want to fight back against Kim!'

'Please just think about it,' Ri said as she hugged Cho again.

Cho never went to meet her at midnight.

SIX

It was the day before the fight and Kim Jong-Un was in his office (which he'd had repurposed into a boxing gym) finishing off some last minute preparations before his flight to Glasgow.

'I – am – going – to – kill – Frank!' he said, spitting out his words between throwing punches at a punch bag with Frank's face on it.

'You're looking well, sir,' Kim's aide said. 'Very well indeed. Frank should pose no problems for you.'

Kim wiped some sweat from his brow then stood with his hands on his hips. 'Pass me a cigar.'

His aide duly obliged, placed a cigar in Kim's mouth and lit it for him.

'Do you think I'll win?' Kim asked.

'Yes, sir. Without a shadow of doubt.'

'That's right,' Kim flexed his muscles in front of the mirror 'Look at me, don't I look like a warrior?'

The aide examined his figure in the reflection. 'Yes. Yes you do,' he lied. He was secretly hoping, to himself of course, that Frank would absolutely leather Kim.

'What intelligence on Mr Frank have you managed to get for me?'

North Korea had a mole in Scotland who was gathering as much info on Frank as he could find. He was a teacher by the name of Eoghann from East Kilbride. Kim Jong-Un's team of researchers had found him on Twitter where he went by the username of 'DPRK Lover'. He was perfect. The man was simply so beige that he would never arouse suspicion.

'Our mole has sent us a dossier on him.' the aide said. 'He has a history of problems with his left knee and is very easy to "wind up" as they say in Scotland.'

'A swift one of these to his leg,' Kim performed a karate chop, 'and he'll crumble to the floor. No match for the legendary Kim Jong-Un.'

'Words could be an effective weapon against him,' the aide said, poring over the dossier. His theory, which he kept to himself of course, was that if Kim wound Frank up enough, Frank would fly into a rage. His disciplinary record at the jail showed a number of 'incidents' with prisoners. The aide could clearly see that Frank was bigger, stronger and fitter than Kim–with just a bit of provocation Frank might take the fight too far and actually kill him.

'I don't need *words*,' Kim said while karate chopping the air furiously. 'I have my hands.' He karate chopped his way towards the big red nuclear button. He swept his hand quickly down towards the button and stopped less than an inch away, the aide let out a small whimper.

'A couple of choice insults could make things... *easier*, sir,' the aide said.

'It sounds to me like you are doubting the raw physicality of Kim Jong-Un, am I correct?'

'N-n-no, sir. I just, I want to help.'

Kim Jong-Un held the aide in a derisory stare.

'I can beat him just fine. The knowledge of his bad knee will be enough to see me through.'

'Very well, sir,' said the aide, trying his best to hide the disappointment in his voice. All he could do now was hope Frank would just rip Kim's head off.

'When do we leave?' Kim asked, pulling on a shirt and trying, but failing, to fasten his cufflinks.

'Tonight, sir.'

•

In Glasgow, Frank's preparations were far more intense than just stripping to his waist and laying into a punch bag. He had a team of physios, dieticians, sports psychologists–not to mention the best fleet of fighting coaches money could buy. Frank was, in every way, shape and form, ready to absolutely fucking leather Kim Jong-Un.

Kim arrived in Scotland the next morning. He strutted through Glasgow Airport in a remarkably ill-fitting tracksuit that Conor McGregor had once worn. He was booed loudly by families heading to Tenerife, stag parties heading to Prague and even by flight attendants and check-in crews. Kim revelled in the hatred. He loved playing the pantomime villain, it was essentially his day job after all.

'The precautionary measures are in place, just in case,' his aide whispered into his ear.

'We won't need them anyway,' Kim said, 'Frank is as good as dead.'

SEVEN

It was the night of the fight. Tickets had sold out within seconds of going on sale. World leaders descended on the SSE Hydro arena in Glasgow, keen to see the historic event unfold. Donald Trump had been vocal on Twitter in support for Frank who he hoped would, 'Destroy the big baby's ass!' Nicola Sturgeon had voiced her astonishment that it was even going ahead. But a midnight home visit from MI6 saw her retract her statement condemning the fight, instead issuing a new one in which she lauded Frank's bravery. Theresa May said something about 'Fields of wheat' and was roundly mocked.

In his dressing room, Frank paced up and down, throwing punches at pads held up by the organiser of the fight, Mark.

'Left,' Mark shouted, 'right, right, DUCK, left. Yes, big man, you're gonnae fuckin kill this cunt.'

'Ahm no countin mah chickens joost yet, mah man. This guy's clearly no aw there. Cin tell he's a bit ae a nutjob, he might be some fighter.'

'Ach away,' Mark scoffed. 'C'mere, look at this.' Mark picked up the remote and turned on the telly in the dressing room. It displayed the ring outside in the arena. Standing in the middle of the ring was Kim Jong-Un, eating what looked like a black pudding supper. Grease was dripping from the paper onto his chest, the glare from the lights accenting his surprisingly ample bosom. As eager fans filed in to take their seats, some hurled insults at Kim. He responded by throwing his chips at them.

'An look at you,' Mark span Frank round so

he was facing the mirror. 'An Adonis.' Over the past fortnight, the tough exercise regime had already turned Frank from just being a unit into an absolute fucking tank.

'Aye,' Frank nodded, 'yer right. Ahm ready fur this. When's the kick aff?'

'Another couple of hours yet, big man. We've got the undercard to go first.'

'Undercard?'

'Fuck, of course. Nae cunt will huv told you aboot that yet. Aw, Frank, mate, just wait til ye hear this. Up first – Ricky Burns versus Alex Salmond. Big Eck's goat the weight advantage but wee Ricky's like lightning, that'll be a good yin. Mhairi Black against Ruth Davidson, that'll be wild. Then finally we've goat Grado up against Willie Rennie. Grado's treatin the whole thing like a laugh but Willie Rennie's deadly serious aboot tryin ae make himself relevant again. It's a wee bit tragic, really.'

Back in the jail, the prisoners were allowed to stay up to watch Frank take on Kim Jong-Un.

'He'll dae it, nae bother,' said Joe taking a seat in front of the telly. 'Embdy want tae stick a wee bet oan?'

'Less of that,' Murray said, standing watch over the prisoners.

'Aw wheesht, you,' Joe whispered to the guy sitting next to him. 'Fuckin grass.'

'What was that?' said Murray walking over to Joe. He'd heard Joe mutter something but couldn't make out what he said. He knew it wouldn't be anything complimentary though. 'You *do* know gambling isn't allowed inside the prison, yeah?'

'And *you* do know that bein a grass isnae allowed either?'

'Excuse me?'

'Grassin me intae the governor cos ae mah phone. Ahm no daft, mate, ah know it wis you.' Joe stood up to his full height and eyeballed Murray.

'Well if Frank had done his job in the first place,' Murray said through tightly clenched teeth. 'I wouldn't have had to *grass* you in.'

'Ye could've joost fuckin left it, ahm no dain any harm.'

'It's against the rules, pal.'

This was like a red rag to a bull for Joe and he snapped. He stuck the head on Murray and the guard hit the deck. Immediately, another two guards jumped on Joe and carted him out of the room.

'That wis well worth it!' he shouted back at Murray. 'Let me know how Frank gets oan, lads!' The guards carted Joe away to solitary, stopping on the way to give him a couple of kickings, just because they could.

In Pyongyang, it was mandatory for every citizen to watch the fight. Cho and her gang squeezed into the city's Hakdanggol Park. Taking a seat next to her pals on the white steps, Cho was buzzing with excitement.

'I can't believe this is actually happening,' Cho

said to Hyang. 'We basically made this happen!'

'It's true, Cho,' Hyang replied, looking not at the giant screen but almost through it. 'I just have a bad feeling about this. I mean, If Kim wins, can you even imagine the ego boost he'll get?'

Cho considered this quietly.

'And,' Hyang continued, 'if he gets beat, who's he going to take it out on?'

'Us,' Cho sighed. She hadn't thought about the possible ramifications of the fight.

'…And now our final undercard fight of the night before the main event,' the announcer's voice boomed around the Hydro. 'It's GRRRRAAAADOOOOOO VERSUS WILLLLLLIIIIIIE RRRRREEEENNNNIE!!!'

The crowd were baying for blood after the previous brutal fights. The bare knuckle format had resulted in burst knuckles and noses galore. The floor of the ring was soaked with blood and the air was thick with the musky smell of sweat.

Grado made his entrance to a chorus of

cheers. He absolutely lapped it up, cupping his ears to the adoring crowd. It was a particularly eclectic mix of people at the fight. World leaders mingled with regular punters, joking about who would win in fights between them. Grado entered the ring and threw off his robe. He slapped his chest and shouted, 'I'm the fuckin man!'

Then the lights went down. The music stopped. The crowd fell silent.

'Ladies and gentlemen,' the announcer boomed once again. 'Please put your hands together for the bad boy of Scottish politics; IT'S WILLLLIIIIE RRRRREEEENNNNIE!'

Willie Rennie strutted through a plume of smoke. The crowd was silent. Willie Rennie's strut dissipated much like the smoke. Nobody cared about him, it was a shame. He walked towards the ring, his shoulders slumped. A lone voice from the crowd shouted its approval.

'On ye go, babe!' It was Willie Rennie's wife. 'Kill the bastard!'

'Thanks, hen,' Willie shouted, waving back. 'I will.'

Willie Rennie climbed into the ring, shrugging off his Lib Dem-yellow robe. The difference between him and Grado was staggering. Grado's shiny, tanned and perfectly smooth torso shimmered under the lights of the Hydro whilst Willie Rennie's gaunt figure skulked about the ring, ribs visible under his pale, languid skin.

'It's yersel, Willie!' Grado said.

'Yes, it is,' replied Willie Rennie.

'Right, boys,' the ref said pulling Grado and Willie Rennie in close to him. 'I'm wanting a good clean fight here. No biting, no scratching, hair pulling, no punches below the belt, okay?'

The two fighters nodded.

'Right, let's go.' The ref pushed the two men apart and stepped out of their way.

'I'm going to kill you,' Willie Rennie said, almost in a whisper, and with a creepy smile.

Grado just laughed and turned round to

share the joke with his team. As he turned his back, the bell rang, and before he could react, Willie Rennie leaped onto his back. The crowd went mental. He wrapped his legs around Grado's waist, locking his ankles together and digging the backs of his heels into Grado's belly. He put his arms under Grado's, reached round and grabbed him by the back of the neck. Grado's arms were now out of action. He span round, desperately trying to free himself of the former Scottish Liberal Democrat leader who had latched onto him, but he couldn't, Willie Rennie had locked on too tightly.

'I'm going to kill you,' seethed Willie Rennie into Grado's ear.

Grado breathed in and out heavily, 'No... fuckin... chance.'

He leaned back and crashed to the floor of the ring. A chorus of 'ooooooh's' filled the arena. Willie Rennie released his grip and Grado stood up. Willie Rennie lay on the floor, gasping for breath. Grado walked over to the ropes and climbed up, shaking a fist in the air in triumph.

'Can you carry on?' the ref asked Willie Rennie, helping him to his feet. Willie Rennie wiped his brow and nodded solemnly. His eyes narrowed on Grado.

'Grado,' he shouted. 'Let's finish this.'

Grado laughed and climbed down off the ropes. 'Moan then,' he said, beckoning Willie Rennie to attack him.

Willie Rennie broke into a run and launched himself at Grado, trying to spear him round the waist. He just bounced off Grado who stood firm and fell to the floor again.

'Get up,' said Grado, hauling him to his feet. Willie Rennie swayed on the spot, looking like he was about to collapse at any second. He looked ready to jump at Grado again but, this time, Grado was ready. As Willie Rennie bent his knees to jump, Grado smashed a fist into his face. The impact broke Willie Rennie's nose with the same ease a sledgehammer would smash through a pane of glass. Willie Rennie was sent flying backwards, crashing to the floor once again as the crowd whooped and cheered for Grado.

After the ring was cleared of Willie Rennie's broken body, it was time for the main event. Frank versus Kim Jong-Un. Frank and Kim sat in their respective dressing rooms. The men would be meeting for the first time in the ring. Frank had been set to do some Conor McGregor style press conferences, full of trash-talking and showboating but Kim had declined.

Frank sat on a chair with his head bowed, going over his planned opening sequence of punches in his head. *Fly oot the traps at the cunt, couple ae jabs roon aboot the heid, then boady, boady, boady an then crack him oan the jaw. He'll go doon like a sack ae shite.*

In his own dressing room, Kim was receiving a neck and shoulder massage from his aide.

'How are you feeling, sir,' the aide asked, working his thumbs into Kim's fatty neck. 'Nervous?'

'No one in my family has ever been nervous,' Kim said, lighting a cigar.

'What is your strategy? You haven't spoken of any great plan to defeat this man?'

Kim puffed on the cigar for a few seconds. 'Intimidation. That's the only weapon I need to win. I'm the leader of the most feared country in the world. Who is he? Who is Frank?' Kim spat out Frank's name as if it tasted horrible in his mouth. 'He's nobody.' Kim shrugged the aide's hands off and stood up.

'Here's your robe, sir,' said the aide. 'Just remember, he has a dodgy left knee.'

Kim pulled it on and looked at his reflection up and down in the mirror. He nodded sagely. The robe was a shimmering, satin, red, white and blue number with pictures of Kim's father and grandfather emblazoned on the back. On the front, sitting proudly, was not the flag of his country, but a big red cartoon version of his nuclear button.

One of the runners poked her head into Kim's dressing room. 'Time for your walk-on.'

'Showtime,' Kim said.

'You're up, Frank,' said Mark. 'Let's fuckin do this.'

Frank jumped to his feet. 'Ahm gonnae leather this cunt.'

'That's mah boy. Aw, eh, before ye go oot there, that wummin fae MI6 wants a word.'

'Wit aboot?'

'Dunno,' Mark checked in the corridor for Katherine. 'Here she comes, mate.'

'Frank, Frank, Frank. Look at you. You're like a Greek god standing there,' said Katherine, breezing into the dressing room.

'Aw cheers, doll,' Frank replied as his cheeks flushed a rosy red colour.

'Not that you'll need it, but I just wanted to wish you good luck. Just remember, you're not just fighting for yourself or for the glory of Scotland, or indeed the UK, but for the people of North Korea. They all want you to win.'

'Frank, you good to go?' a runner asked. 'Kim's walking on first, then you.'

'Sound, pal. Let's do this.'

'Ladies and gentlemen,' said the announcer as the lights dimmed in the stadium. 'Please welcome to the ring the most feared dictator in the world, a man who has executed over 300 people in the last 7 years, a man who runs the most secretive and dangerous regime on Earth, the leader of North Korea, it's KIM JOOONG-UUUUUUNN!' Kim's favourite song (Brother Louie by Modern Talking) kicked in and Kim appeared through the smoke.

A lot of fighters liked to strut their way to the ring, some bounced along throwing punches at the air, some danced–Kim walked to the ring like he was walking to the bottom of his garden to have a look for something in his shed; purposeful but laid-back. He was still puffing on his cigar and smiling broadly. The baying crowd booed and hissed at him as he walked by.

'You're gonna get your ass handed to you, Kim!' Donald Trump shouted to him from the front row. Kim cupped his ears at him and laughed before throwing his cigar at Trump. Trump's bodyguards had to restrain him as he flailed around, trying to get to Kim. It was obvious that Kim was loving all the attention. He stood in the ring with his arms outstretched, drinking in all the hate and vitriol being fired at him. He took off his robe and flung it into the crowd.

'And now, here is the contender. The man going toe-to-toe with Kim Jong-Un. He's the most respected guard in Scotland's toughest jail. He's confronted murderers, rapists, paedos and armed robbers every single day for the last 10 years. He's FRANK 'THE KILLER' CURRRRAAAAN!'

This time the crowd were whooping and cheering. Frank strode towards the ring with a spring in his step. His arms already twitching, desperate to throw a punch at Kim Jong-Un's face. He high-fived Will Smith who was sitting next to Trump. Nicola Sturgeon gave him a thumbs up and a smile that seemed to say, 'Go and fuckin leather that cunt.'

Frank and Kim stood diagonally opposite each other in the ring. Kim leaned back into the ropes, receiving another last minute massage from his aide. Frank's coaches whispered encouragement into his ear.

'Just remember the plan, Frank,' his head coach said. 'Get him down as quick as. He'll be able to take a good few hits so we need to get him knocked out before he tires you out.'

'Nae problem,' Frank said, making eye contact with Kim who just grinned back at him.

DINGDINGDING

Frank did as he planned. He sprang at Kim right from the off, unleashing a hail of punches at the dictator's face. With a right hook, he punched Kim in the left eye and it instantly swelled. With a left hook, he got him square on the nose, flattening it. Already, Frank's knuckles were red raw and bruised, but he kept going until the referee pulled him away from Kim.

Kim wiped some blood away from his mouth and laughed at Frank.

'Come ahead,' he said.

Frank did as he was invited and advanced on Kim again. He flung a quick left jab, hoping to get Kim's other eye out of action but he weaved out of the way and laughed again. He bounced on the spot and the atmosphere in the stadium changed. It looked like this wouldn't be the walkover for Frank everyone had thought it would be.

•

In Pyongyang, Cho watched on, stunned at the agility of Kim Jong-Un as he dodged everything Frank threw at him.

'I can't watch,' Hyang said, covering his eyes. 'If Kim gets one good punch in, Frank will go down, he's exhausted already. Kim's hardly broke a sweat.'

'It'll be okay,' said Cho, trying her best to sound positive. 'Just watch.'

DINGDINGDING

The fighters went back to their corners. Kim laughing and Frank raging.

'How the fuck's he so quick,' Frank moaned to the coaches. 'Cunt's duckin and divin like a fuckin cat. Ah cannae get near him.'

'It's easy to avoid blows when you know they're coming, mate,' his coach said, mopping Frank's brow. 'You need to be more… unpredictable.'

'How'd ye mean?'

'Stick the nut oan him,' Mark said, making an appearance. 'Anyhin goes in a fight like this. Pin him doon or suhin. Yer bein too fancy, tryin ae be aw Mayweathery. This isnae fuckin Mike Tyson yer up against. Or even a cunt fae the jail.

He's a naebody. He's no even landed a punch oan you yet and he's already goat ye beat up here,' Mark stabbed a finger at Frank's forehead.

'Right,' Frank nodded. 'Aye, yer right.' He stood up and faced the crowd. 'FUCKIN MOAN THEN!' he roared and the crowd roared back.

DINGDINGDING

This time Frank sauntered over to Kim, who had his fists up trying to block punches that didn't arrive.

'Fuckin state ae this cunt,' Frank shouted at the crowd, pointing at Kim.

Kim Jong-Un saw his chance while Frank was distracted by the adoring crowd and karate chopped Frank's knee.

'Aw, ya cunt,' Frank hopped away. Kim howled with laughter.

'Ye awrite, big man?' Mark shouted over.

'He goat mah gammy knee, the prick.'

'STICK THE NUT OAN HIM!'

Frank composed himself and tried not to think about the pain pulsing in his knee. Kim

81

leaned back against the ropes and patted his enormous belly.

'Too easy,' Kim laughed. 'Far too easy.'

Frank ran towards Kim, his knee almost buckled under him with every step and the throbbing agony was making his eyes water but he powered through. He grabbed Kim by the curtains of black hair which lay either side of his face, drew his neck back, pulled Kim towards him, and threw his head downwards. Frank's forehead connected with the bridge of Kim's already broken nose in a sickening clash of bone. Kim slumped to the floor. The crowd were on their feet screaming with joy. Frank staggered backwards and collapsed into his corner.

The feed Cho was watching in North Korea had roughly a 20 second delay. Frank was just about to land a belter of a heider on Kim Jong-Un when the screen turned off. Armed police raised their guns at the crowd as they showed their disapproval. One of the policemen's radios crackled into life.

'Affirmative,' he said into it. 'Kim Jong-Un

won by a knockout,' he announced to the crowd. 'Return to your homes. We'll show the rest of the fight on the TV tomorrow night.'

'Shit,' Hyang said dejectedly. 'I can't believe this. The bastard won.'

'We were foolish to believe in this charade,' Cho said. Her expressionless face stared at the police as they corralled people out of the park. 'As if they would allow us to know if he was beaten. I don't know why I allowed myself to get so carried away. I don't even know why I bother with our stupid group.'

'Cho, please,' Hyang pleaded. But it was too late. Cho had stormed off and was indistinguishable within the sea of the bodies heading for the exits.

'… And the winner, by a knockout, is FRANK 'THE KILLLLLLLLLLLEEEEER' CURRAN!'

The ref raised Frank's hand in the air as Kim's aide dragged his unconscious body out of the ring.

Frank climbed up and stood on the top rope,

punching the air in jubilation.

'Way to go, buddy,' Donald Trump said, coming over to congratulate Frank.

'You get tae fuck unless yer wantin a fight anaw.'

'Hey, you can't speak to me like that. You wanna fight? I'll give ya a fight, buddy! I'll give you the best fight of your life. I'm the best fighter in this room. In this damn country!'

Trump's bodyguards had to quieten him down once again and pull him away.

'You are the best fighter,' one of them whispered in his ear while smoothing down his hair to soothe him. 'The best in aaaaall the land, little buddy. Let's go and get you a KFC. Would you like that?'

'Frank, how does it feel?' a reporter asked. A million other microphones were thrust in his face.

'Eh, magic.'

'And Frank, what next?'

'Fuck knows, man. Ah wis sacked the other

week so, eh, joost keep fightin ah hink.'

'Who will your next opponent be?'

'Ah'll say Putin,' Frank grabbed a mic and stared straight down one of the many TV cameras. 'Vlad! You're fuckin gettin it! Hink yer a hard man cause yer fae Russia? Ah've done harder shites than you, pal.'

'Right you, fur fuck sake,' said Mark, pulling him away from the journalists. 'The fuckin KGB will be payin ye a visit if ye don't calm doon.'

'Sorry, ah goat a bit carried away.'

'Yer next fight's lined up awready.'

'Aye? Who is it?'

'Willie Rennie,' Mark led Frank out of the ring and back to his dressing room to clean up, 'the wee man's desperate fur another fight. He's scared me a wee bit, truth be told. Look at this.'

Mark opened a door to his right. Willie Rennie was restrained in a dolly. The veins in his neck bulging under his skin like lengths of copper piping as he tried to free himself from his restraints. His voice was muffled under the

Hannibal-style mask he was wearing but Frank was sure he could make out that he was saying, 'I'm going to kill you.'

EIGHT

The next night in Pyongyang, Cho sat deflated on her uncomfortable couch. The state had just shown the remainder of the previous night's fight. Or rather, their version. As Frank was about to stick the heid on Kim Jong-Un, some poorly executed CGI made it look as if Kim dodged the blow. Then it cut to what was clearly a pair of lookalikes trading blows in a shoddily-made film studio boxing ring, before the fake Kim landed a weak punch on the fake Frank's chin and knocked him out. Then, the real Kim was shown in his dressing room, celebrating wildly in scenes which had clearly been filmed before the fight as Kim's nose and eye were both completely unharmed.

'Let this be a message to the world, and also to my people,' Kim stated to the camera. 'I am invincible.'

Cho switched her telly off and sat for a moment in silence. Everything was finished. Her determination and passion for the resistance movement had been knocked out of her. It was game over. There was nothing she could do now. Kim would come down hard on anyone who had openly doubted him. Her group would be disbanded, no doubt, not just out of fear but because they had been demoralised. In fact, Cho wouldn't be surprised if she was paid a visit from the secret police any day/minute now.

As this thought floated through her head, she was startled by a loud knocking on her door.

Surely they wouldn't have come for her so soon. However, Cho was ready to accept her fate–she had tried and failed to take down the regime. What else was there left to live for?

She opened the door, ready to face whatever awaited her, be it the barrel of a gun or a bag being thrown over her head.

She was instead greeted by a tiny, elderly, white-haired, bespectacled man.

'Cho?' he asked tentatively.

Cho nodded, looking at the parcel in the man's hands.

'I have something for you. A gift.'

'A gift?' Cho was confused.

'Yes, a gift. From a friend in the south,' the old man smiled and offered her the parcel. Cho took it from him gingerly.

The old man winked and shuffled away down the hall.

Cho closed the door behind him. The parcel was a white padded envelope, wrapped in brown tape and with Cho's name and address written on it in neat handwriting. She took it into her kitchen and grabbed a pair of scissors.

Cho slid the blade under the flap on the back of the parcel and cut away at the tape. Her excitement made her abandon the scissors and rip it open like a child at Christmas.

Inside, there was something wrapped in a plastic bag. She unwrapped it and found a video tape and a letter.

Written on the tape was 'Kim v Frank–uncut'. Cho laughed and read the letter:

Dearest Cho,

Please use the video to help the cause.

Keep fighting the good fight and stay safe.

Your friend,

Ri x

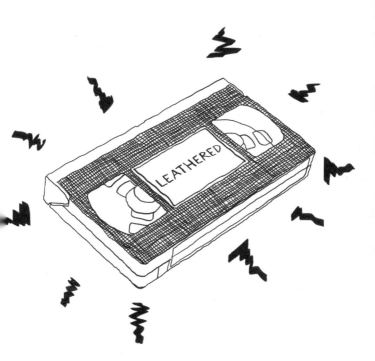